Olly and Me

For Vanessa and Allan

First U.S. edition 2004

Library of Congress Cataloging-in-Publication Data is available.

Library of Congress Catalog Card Number 2003055088

ISBN 0-7636-2374-1

2 4 6 8 10 9 7 5 3 1

Printed in China

This book was typeset in Stempel Schneidler.
The artwork for this book was painted in gouache color and oil pastels and finished with fine brushes.

Candlewick Press
2067 Massachusetts Avenue
Cambridge, Massachusetts 02140

visit us at www.candlewick.com

Olly and Me

Shirley Hughes

CANDLEWICK PRESS
CAMBRIDGE, MASSACHUSETTS

Three in a Bed

Three in a bed
Under the covers,
Bemily, me,
And Olly, my brother.
He's at one end,
We're at the other,
Warm in bed
Under the covers.

Ice in the Park

It's cold in the park, cold, cold,
And the wind blows sharp and keen.
The path's frosted over,
White as chalk.
Too cold to stand still,

Too cold to walk,
Better to run,
Better to shout,

Holler and wave your arms about,
See your breath come out like steam.

There's ice on the lake,
So the ducks can't swim;
Only one little hole for diving in.
It's cold in the park, cold, cold;
No more leaves on the tree.
It's almost too cold for the hungry birds,
And too cold for Olly and me.

Olly Joins In

I'm doing ballet! With Amanda and James and Kim
and Norah. I've got special pink dancing shoes
and white tights and a sticking-out skirt.

When the music plays, we stand in a row and
bend our knees and point our toes—this way,
then this way. We stretch up our arms
and dance about.

The moms and dads and grannies sit on chairs and watch.
And Olly watches too, sitting on Mom's lap.

Once, when we were being spring flowers coming
out of the ground, Olly joined in and tried
to dance too!

Olly doesn't know how to dance properly yet.
I didn't much like it when he joined in.
But nobody else seemed to mind.

Pancakes

When Mom goes out and Dad looks after us, we often do the cooking. Making pancakes with Dad is quite exciting. He cracks open the eggs, and Olly and I help him stir the batter. Then Dad cooks them in a pan.

The most exciting part is when he picks up the pan and flips the pancake into the air and catches it. It is even more exciting when he misses and some of the pancake goes on the floor.

Our dog, Buster, likes that. But eating pancakes with plenty of syrup is the part we like best of all.

My Friend Betty

There's a place in the park where the farm animals live: the pig with a house of his own, and the hens and geese. But whenever we go there, I always visit Betty the sheep first.

She has a nice fat back. And when she sees me, she always turns her head and lets me touch her nose.

Olly likes rabbits.

When they come out of their hutch, we're allowed to stroke
them—the beautiful black one, the brown ones with
silky ears, and the white one with pink eyes.

But Betty
is my special friend.

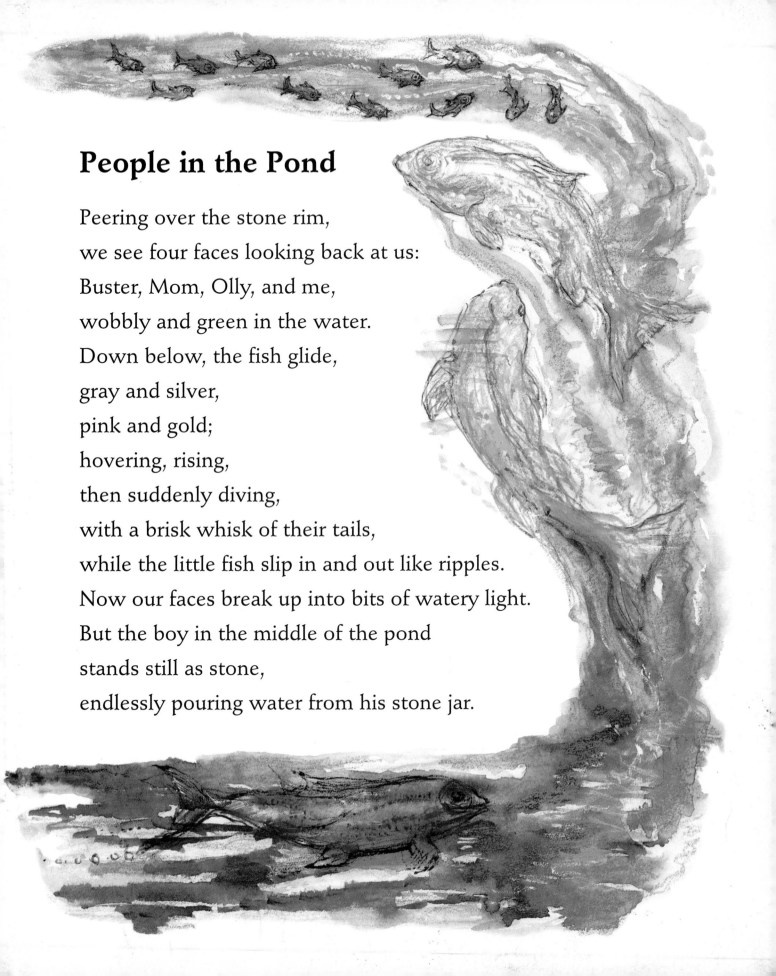

People in the Pond

Peering over the stone rim,
we see four faces looking back at us:
Buster, Mom, Olly, and me,
wobbly and green in the water.
Down below, the fish glide,
gray and silver,
pink and gold;
hovering, rising,
then suddenly diving,
with a brisk whisk of their tails,
while the little fish slip in and out like ripples.
Now our faces break up into bits of watery light.
But the boy in the middle of the pond
stands still as stone,
endlessly pouring water from his stone jar.

Car Ride

We're in the car,

Strapped in our seats.

We sit and we sit,

Looking at other cars

And the backs of trucks.

Olly is cross,

Bemily's feeling sick,

As we watch the streetlights

Gliding past—fast!

Like people in a long, long line.

And still we sit.

Olly sucks his thumb

And dozes off.

I've got my book

But I still look

At the huge billboards

(Which I can't read)

And the places for gas,

And the streetlights,

Rushing past.

And I wish and I wish we were there.

Then, at last,
We stop!
Olly wakes up
(Still cross)
But we're there!
We're there, in the bright air!
And we're walking on grass.

Fireworks

Hoisted up on shoulders so I can see,

We're out late, just Dad and me,

And I'm hugging his head in the warm blue dark

As we crane our necks by the lake in the park.

And rockets whoosh through the summer night,

Trailing their tails of glittering light,

Cutting up, up, up across the sky,

Exploding in stars, impossibly high;

And golden fountains pour out showers

Of shimmering rain, like fiery flowers;

Pinwheels whiz around and around,

Roman candles light the ground,

As I stop my ears and gasp and gaze

At a lake on fire and a sky ablaze.

Splishing and Splashing

Deep in the green shade
Two moms sit, lazily chatting.

But Norah and I are busy,
Turning the tap,
Filling buckets
And the watering can,
Slooshing in it;
Making mud,
Making rivers and dams
And swimming pools for ants.

Olly's busy too,
Sitting in a basin of water,
Bailing out.

Our Cat, Ginger

No cat is as nice as
our cat, Ginger.

There's the sleek black
cat with pale green eyes
that we often talk to
on our way to the park,

and there's the big
striped Daddy cat
who lives next door.

There are four little kittens
at my friend Norah's house.

And there's Grandma's beautiful Queenie.

But no cat—*no* cat—is as nice
as our cat, Ginger.

Saturday Shopping

Saturday is a shopping day.
Olly and I don't like shops much,
but we like the market
when the stalls are all lit up,
and there are crowds of people.
I hold on tight to Dad's hand
while we load Olly's stroller
with apples, grapes, and bananas
and sometimes even a pumpkin.
There are squeaky toys
and plastic balls,
T-shirts, watches, and sparkling rings.
And you can smell the smell from the baker's shops,
bread, cakes, cookies, and hot pies,
tempting us in from the dark street.

Stories Galore

Olly and I have lots of books.
Olly likes chewing his, but he stops doing it
when I show him the pictures.
Down at the library there are stories galore.
We go there on Saturday afternoons.

While Mom is choosing her book, Dad and Olly
and I sit on cushions on the floor while a lady
tells us all about the Three Little Pigs and the
Owl and the Pussycat and the Billy Goats Gruff.
And Olly sits still and listens without wriggling
(well, most of the time, anyway).

When it's time for me to choose my books to take
home, Dad says, "Why do you always choose
the same ones?" And I say it's because
I like them best, of course.
But one day I will read
all the books in the library!

Old Bones

At the Natural History Museum,
in the biggest room of all,
there's a huge skeleton.

It is of an animal who lived long ago, as big as a ship from head to tail, with a great arched neck and holes where once there were eyes.

And when Olly and I are standing under its tail, looking at its great teeth, I wonder what it would be like to meet an alive one.

But Dad says there were no people living in the world then.

Luckily.

Happy Birthday, Dear Mom

I'm coloring a beautiful card for Mom.
Because tomorrow, when she wakes up, it will be
her birthday! I've tried to explain to Olly about birthdays,
but he doesn't quite understand. He can't remember
his own, but he's hoping for balloons. They are
his favorite thing at the moment.

I've got a present for Mom that
Dad and I bought together.
It's a key ring with a sheep on
it, so she won't have to search
for her keys so often.

We've got a surprise cake
with candles. (But not one for every
year because Dad says
that grownups don't
always have that.)

Tomorrow Mom will have breakfast in bed.
There will be lots of crushy hugs. And presents.

Buster will have

a meaty treat.

Ginger will wear a blue bow on her
collar, which she will try to take off.

Grandpa and Grandma will come.

And after Mom has blown out her cake candles
we'll all sing "Happy Birthday, Dear Mom!"

And even Olly, in Olly language, will join in.